Why So Sad, Brown Rabbit?

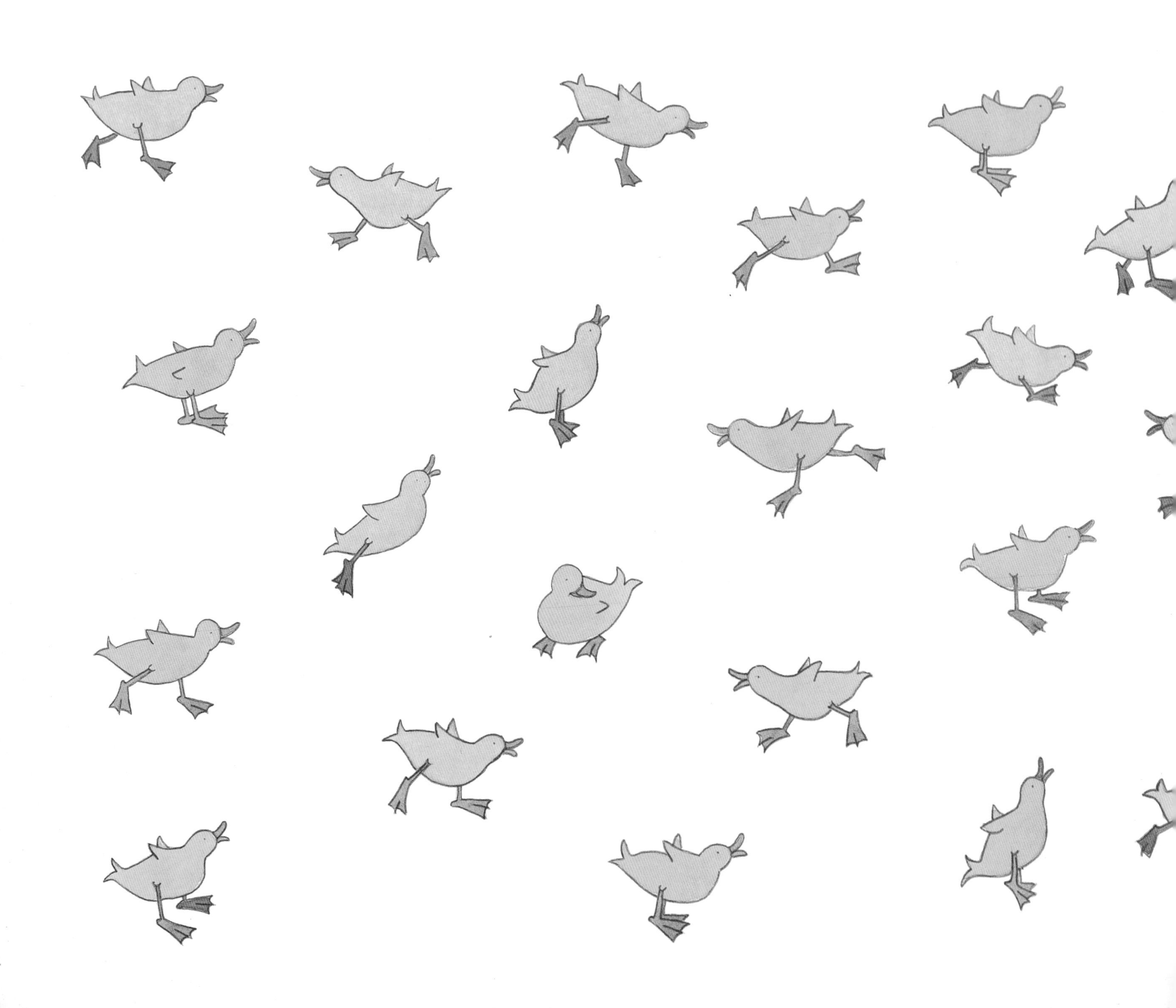

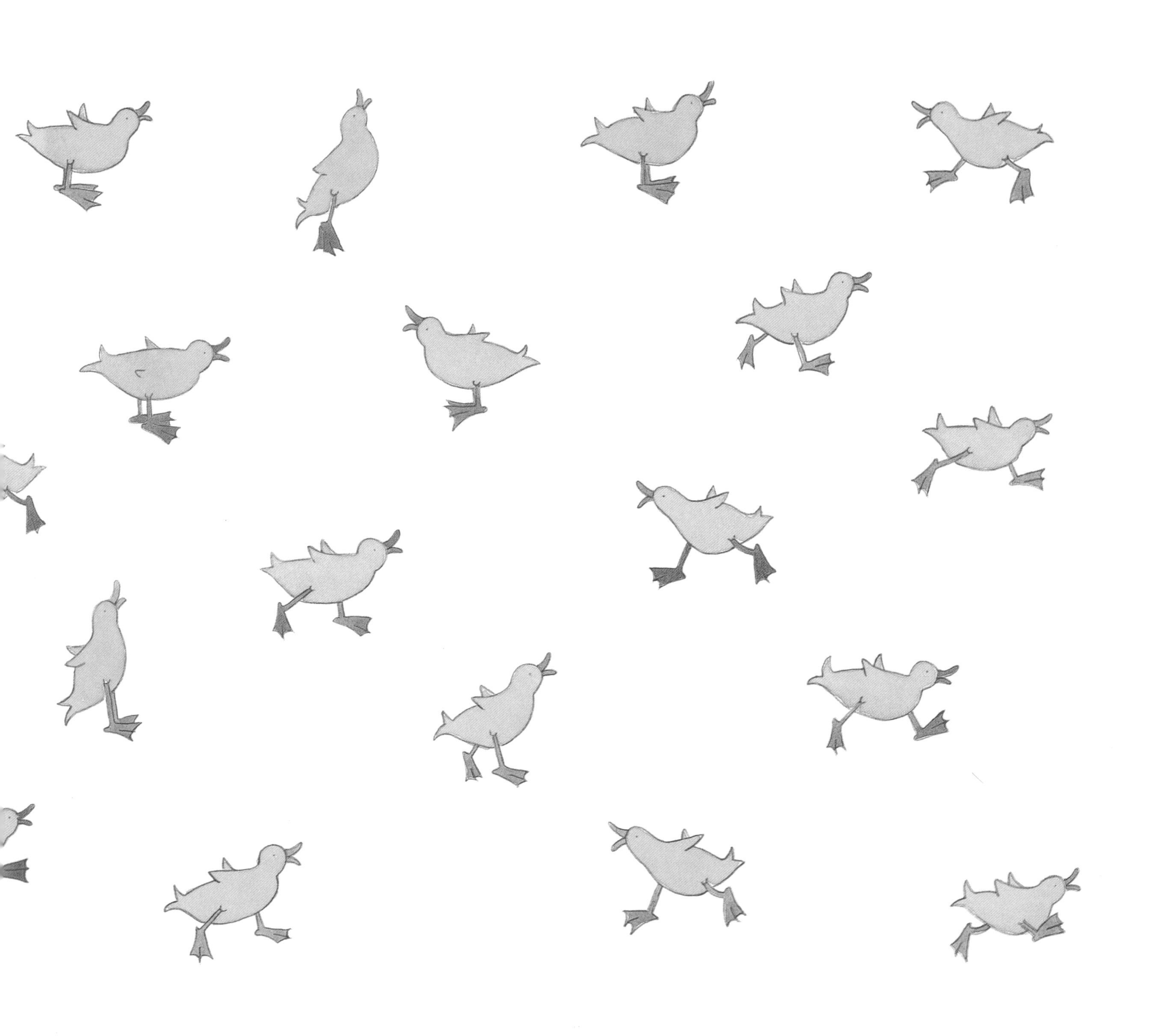

FOR Hilary
S.C.

FOR Sue, Jana & Graham
J.K.

This paperback edition published in 1998

First published in 1998 by Magi Publications
22 Manchester Street, London WIM 5PG

Printed in Belgium by Proost NV, Turnhout

ISBN 1 85430 452 6

Why So Sad, Brown Rabbit?

BY

Sheridan Cain

ILLUSTRATED BY

Jo Kelly

Spring had come at last and all the rabbits were
playing hop, skip and jump around the meadow.
But watching from the edge, with his ears all
droopy, sat Brown Rabbit.

"What's wrong, Brown Rabbit?" asked Grey Mouse. "Why so sad on such a lovely day?"

"I wish I could hop, skip and jump, too," said Brown Rabbit. "But I'm too old to play games."
"If only you had a family," said Grey Mouse. "Then you could teach your children to play games. That would be just as much fun."

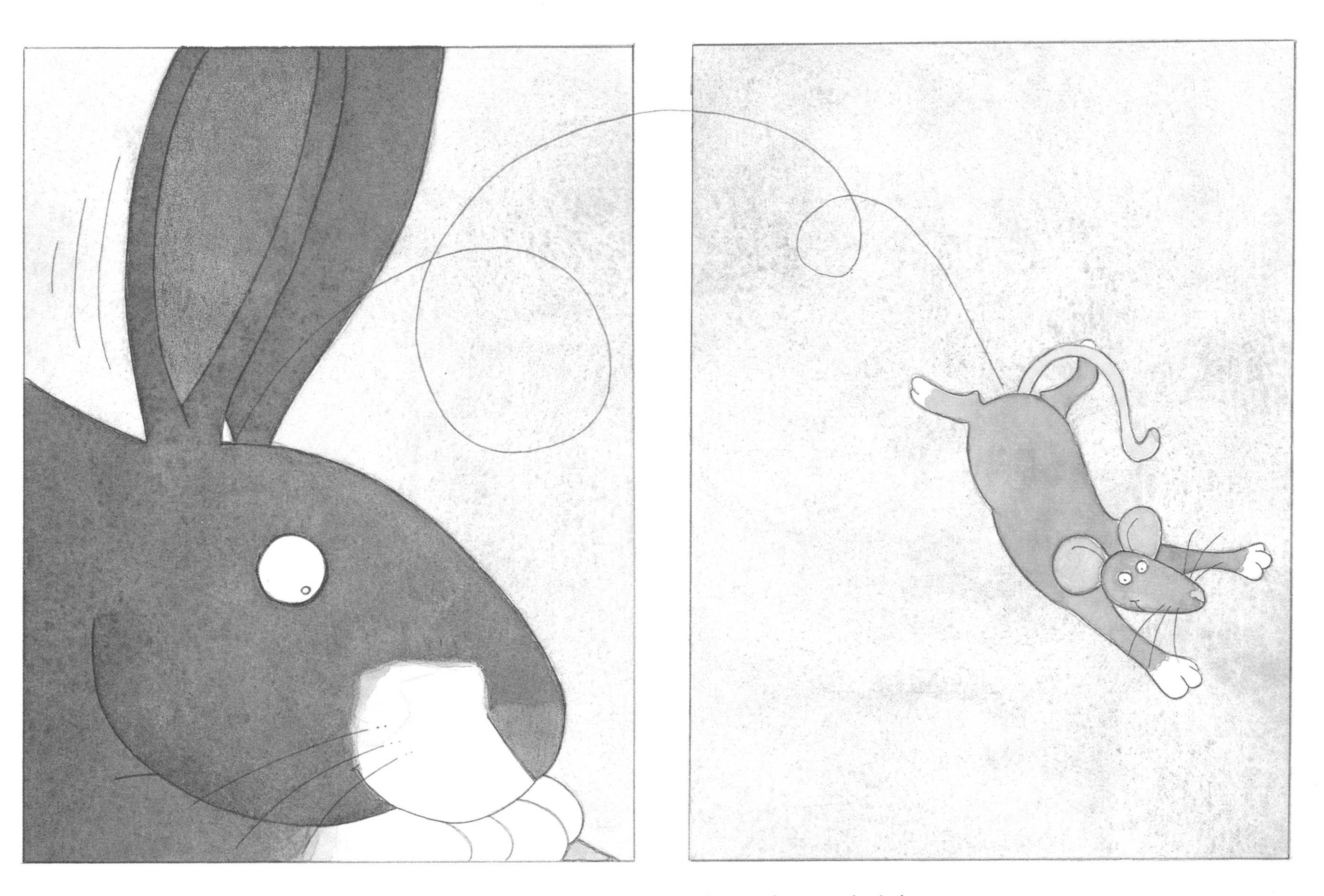

Brown Rabbit's spirits lifted and so did his ears,
sending Grey Mouse flying.
"That's a wonderful idea," said Brown Rabbit,
helping the little mouse to his feet. "I must find
a wife at once."

Brown Rabbit set off that very day.
He hopped across fields . . .

and he hopped through woods . . .

and he hopped over hills, but he didn't
meet one suitable lady rabbit anywhere.

Brown Rabbit was tired
and his feet were sore.

He stopped by a barn and
rested on a pile of hay.

Very soon, he was fast asleep.

Brown Rabbit woke with a start.
What was wrong?

Something was wiggling and
jiggling under the hay.

He looked down and saw three eggs.

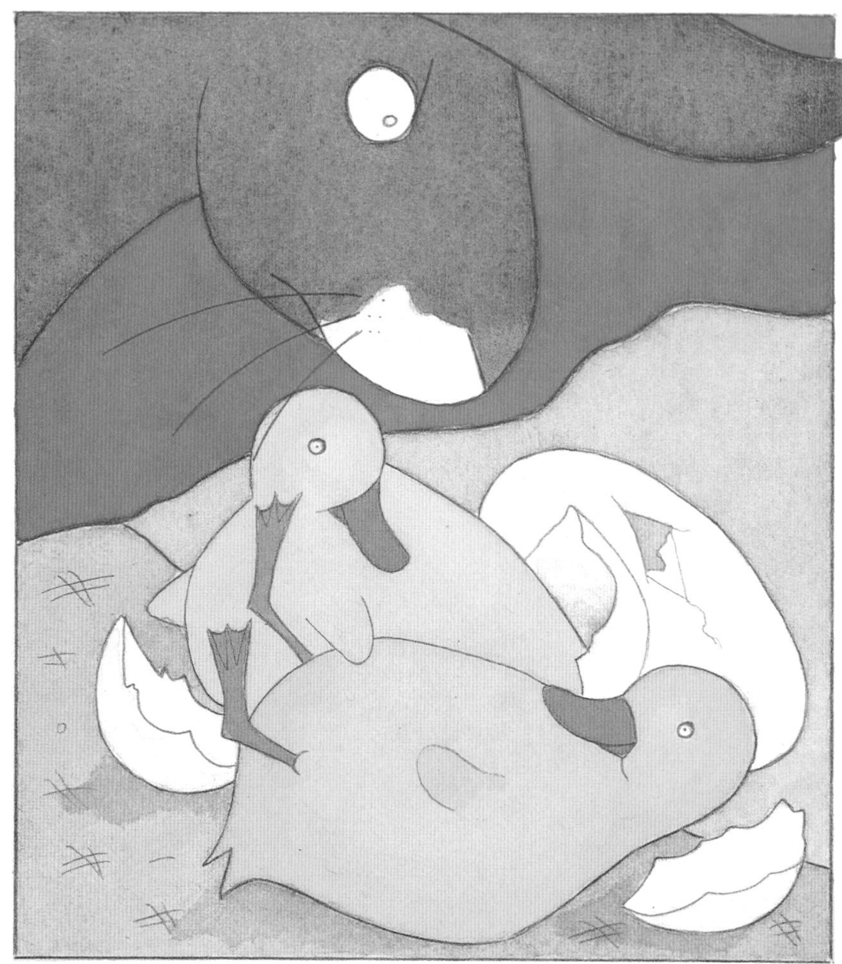

As Brown Rabbit watched, one of the eggs
began to crack.
A tiny beak appeared, then a tiny wet head.
The egg fell apart and out stepped a little
duckling.
There was another crack, and another . . .

and now there were three little ducklings,
all standing in a row.
"Mama!" they quacked, looking straight at
Brown Rabbit.
"Oh dear, I'm not your mama," said Brown
Rabbit in dismay. But it was no good.
"MAMA, MAMA," they quacked again.

"Don't worry, little ducklings," said Brown Rabbit. "I'll help you find your mama."
He set off towards the farmyard and the ducklings waddled after him.

Very soon they met Porker Pig.
"Hello," said Brown Rabbit. "These little fellows have lost their mama. Have you seen her?"
"No ducks round here," snorted Porker, and without another word, she carried on eating her breakfast.

Brown Rabbit thumped his feet. He thought
Porker was very unhelpful, so he hopped
away towards the pond.
"MAMA!" cried the ducklings, trying to keep
up with him.

Very soon they met White Swan.
"Hello," said Brown Rabbit. "These little fellows want their mama. Have you seen her?"
"Certainly not!" hissed White Swan. "This is my pond. I don't allow silly old ducks to clutter it." He turned his back on Brown Rabbit and the ducklings and glided silently away.

"Thank you for nothing," said Brown Rabbit crossly. He hopped on into the farmyard and the ducklings hurried along behind him.
"MAMA!" they cried. "Wait for us!"
Brown Rabbit slowed down so they could keep up.

Right in front of him was Cackly Hen.
"Hello," said Brown Rabbit. "These little fellows need their mama. Have you seen her anywhere?"
"Cluck, cluck, you're out of luck," said Cackly, pecking at some corn. "All the ducks left yesterday."

Brown Rabbit sat down.
"What shall I do?" he said miserably. He looked at the three sad little faces. "You're all alone, just like me."
"MAMA!" cried the ducklings and snuggled up close.

Brown Rabbit suddenly felt better.
"How about a game?" he said. "That will cheer you up." The little ducklings' faces lit up, so Brown Rabbit taught them . . .

how to hop . . .

and how to skip . . .

and how to jump.

What fun they had!

"MAMA!" cried the ducklings in excitement. "MAMA!"
"Oh please don't call me Mama," said Brown Rabbit.

"PAPA!" cried the ducklings.
"PAPA!"
Brown Rabbit smiled.
"Hurray!" cheered Grey Mouse.
"You've found your family at last!"

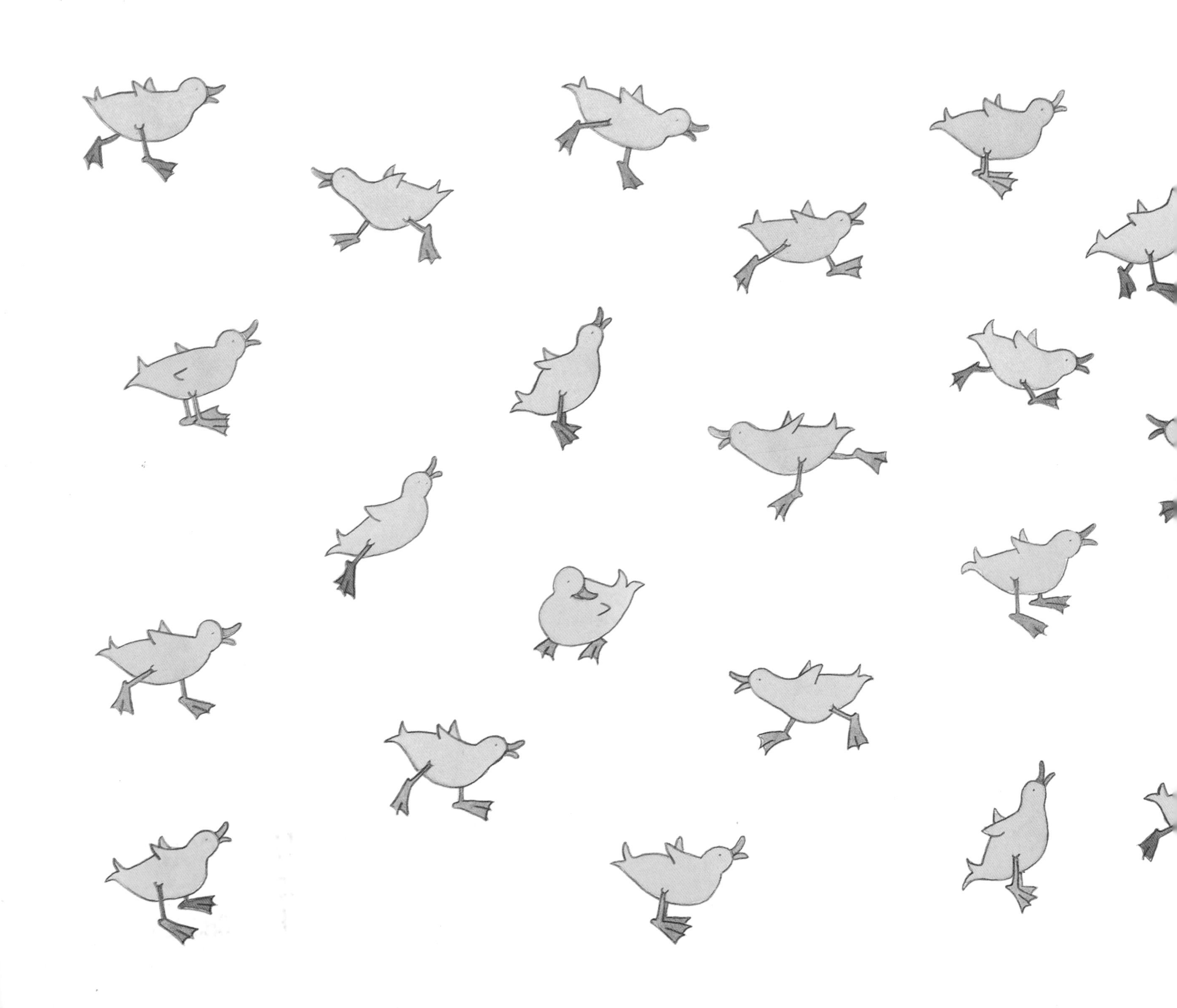

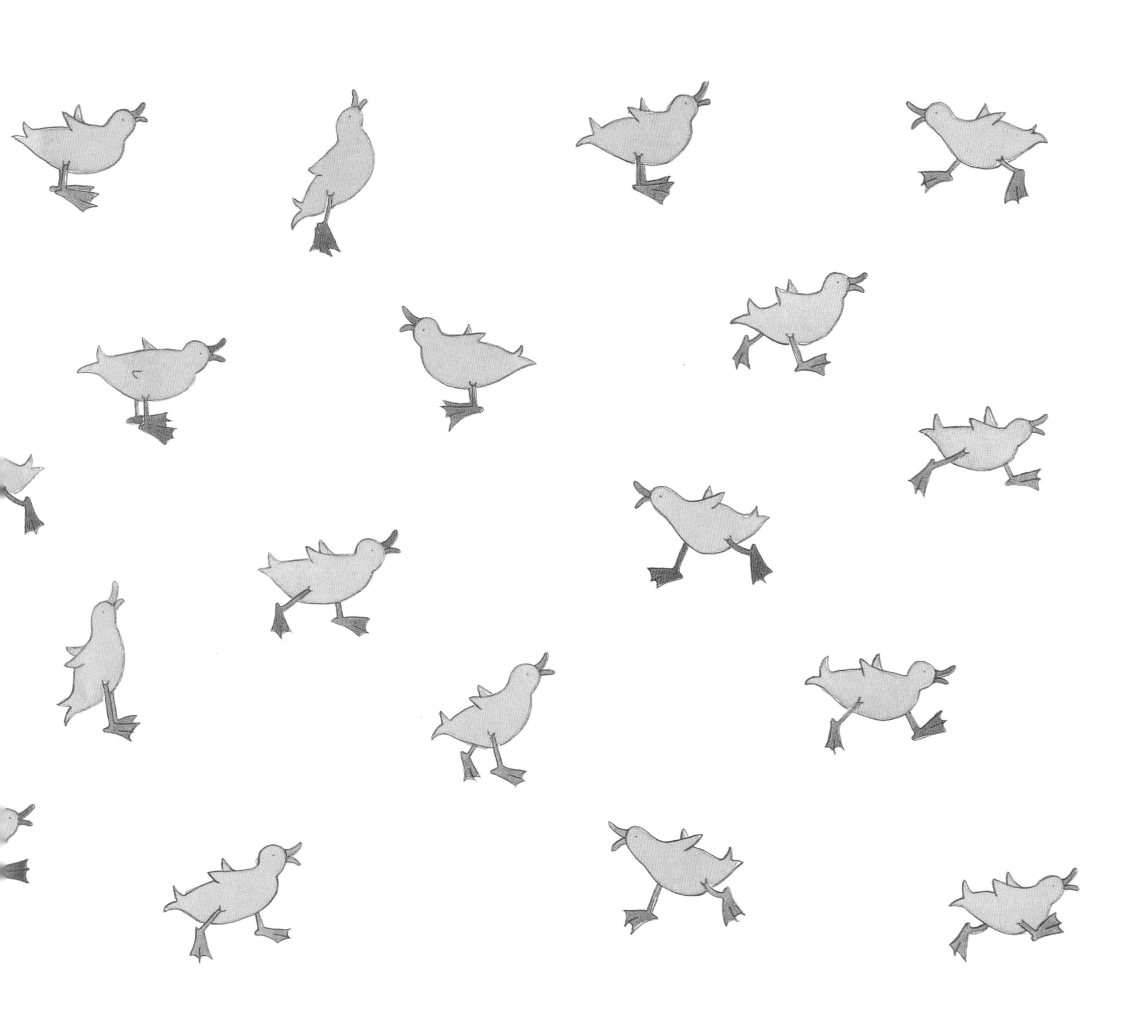